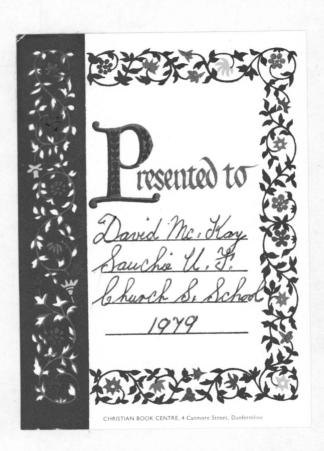

Presented to

David Mc. Kay
Sauchie U. F.
Church S. School
1979

CHRISTIAN BOOK CENTRE, 4 Canmore Street, Dunfermline

THE SECRET OF
THE FOREST HUT

THE SECRET
OF THE
FOREST HUT

By
EDNA O. MENZIES

LONDON
PICKERING & INGLIS LTD.
1972

PICKERING & INGLIS LTD.
29 LUDGATE HILL, LONDON, E.C.4
26 BOTHWELL STREET, GLASGOW, G2 6PA

Printed in Great Britain by A. McLay & Co. Ltd., Cardiff

Lovingly dedicated
to my mother with grateful thanks for her
interest and prayers throughout the years
for the boys and girls of Africa

CONTENTS

The Mystery Begins

1   DANIYA TOOK UP HIS SHORT-HANDLED hoe and started toward the peanut patch.

"Hurry up, Deeja," he called. "We must go at once or the sun will be hot upon us before we have finished our work."

"I am coming," answered his twin as she slipped out of the round, mud hut, and picking up her hoe, she sped down the path after her brother.

The sturdy, brown bodies of the twelve year old twins moved easily over the narrow trail. The warm sand squished squashed between their bare toes and slid quietly away from their hurrying feet. Deeja was a little shorter than her brother, but their round, good-natured faces were almost identical. 'As like as two gourds on the one vine', their father often teased.

The trail wound its way in and out between the small farms. Here and there, scrawny, brown goats grazed in the shade of old baobob trees. On the large flat rocks, bright gold and blue lizards blinked lazily in the hot African sunshine. In the distance, a young Fulani boy herded his cattle. The plaintive notes from his cornstalk flute drifted gently over the valley.

"I just can't understand it," Deeja said as she trotted along behind her brother. "We have been at our new school two weeks now and the children are as unfriendly as ever."

"Truly," Daniya agreed. "And not only that but very few of them come out to Sunday School. Our father explains things so clearly I'm sure they could understand, if they would only come and let the pleasant words sink into their hearts."

"Kai!" Deeja exclaimed as a small grey mouse suddenly scuttled across her foot and plunged to safety in the crevice of a nearby rock.

Daniya turned quickly. "What was it?"

Deeja chuckled. "Only a mouse. But fear has taken away all its sense. It —" she paused. Then she continued soberly, "It scurried off just like the girls and boys do in this village every time we go near them. They seem afraid of us, Daniya."

"They certainly do." Daniya took a vicious swipe with his hoe at a tall weed as they reached the peanut patch. "I've tried for days to make friends with Toma but he acts as if he is afraid to be seen with me."

"That's just how his sister, Binta, is with me," Deeja sighed as she bent over and began to hoe.

They worked silently for awhile. But as their hoes flashed in and out of the hard, red earth their thoughts were busy. They had been so happy when their father, Pastor Bako, had been sent to this village of Dadin-Wanda-Ya-Je. The name of the village meant 'happiness for all who go there' and they had all felt sure it would be a nice place to live. When Deeja had heard the name she had remarked, "Even if the people don't know happiness yet, they will find it when they accept the pleasant news of the Saviour."

'But how can they accept the good news if they won't come and listen to it,' Daniya thought now as he straightened up and wiped the perspiration from his forehead. Then he said, "Do you know what I think, Deeja? I think there is someone working against us in this place."

Deeja dropped her hoe and stared at her brother. "Well, of course, we know Satan will try and hinder us. But . . ."

"I mean a human being," Daniya interrupted. "Someone living right in this village who has already warned the school kids not to be friends with us."

Deeja nodded. "I think you're right. Have you any idea who it is?"

"Not yet," Daniya said. "But I mean to find out."

The sun blazed fiercely as it climbed higher and higher. Little beads of moisture glistened on the children's foreheads and ran in tiny trickles down their cheeks. Fortunately the peanut patch wasn't a large one and by noon the last row was done and the twins started for home.

As they walked they sang,

"Jesus, Jesus You are our Captain

You will give us victory in the fight."

Suddenly a boy stepped out of the tall grass by the roadside and barred their way. Tattered blue trousers clung to his lanky form. Thrown over his shoulders and knotted at the neck hung a dirty white sweater. A small-brimmed straw hat sat at a jaunty angle on his curly head. He stared at the twins for a minute. Then he folded his arms and laughed mockingly.

"Well, well!" he said. "If it isn't the preacher's kids. Don't tell me you've been working at the farm? Beyond doubt I thought you were just useless ones like your father."

11

"Our father . . ." Deeja began indignantly.

But Daniya interrupted her quietly. "Our father is not useless. He has come to your village with a message from the King."

"A king?" The boy's voice was sceptical. "What king would send his message with a meddlesome preacher?"

"Jesus is the King of kings and Lord of lords," Daniya's voice was reverent. "Jesus has sent our father to tell you the way to Heaven."

"Is that so?" The boy leaned forward threateningly. "Well let me tell you this right now. My name is Buba." He pointed to his chest and seemed to swell visibly. "And any of those school kids who start following your 'Jesus Way' will have to answer to me, see?

"There's another thing that you had better tell your father too," he continued. "The people of this village prefer the way of the forest hut. My uncle is in charge of it. We will never leave our way for yours. So you may as well pack up at once."

"What's in the forest hut?" Deeja asked.

Buba's dark eyes gleamed. "That is a secret. And you needn't think that any useless ones will ever discover it either." The next moment he had pushed them roughly aside and swaggered off down the trail.

"He makes himself big, that one," Deeja said as they started off once more. "I wonder what is inside the hut that is such a big secret?"

"I don't know," Daniya answered. "But I do know they worship evil spirits there."

"Yes, we all know they do that," Deeja agreed. "I do wish, though, that we knew the secret of where their hut is and what's inside it."

12

Daniya was silent. His brows were drawn together in a deep frown. Suddenly he stopped short. "That's it, Deeja. He's the one!"

"He's the one, what?" Deeja asked.

"Buba is the one who is hindering us of course," Daniya answered. "Didn't he say that if any of the school kids followed the 'Jesus Way' they would have to answer to him?"

Deeja nodded. "Yes, and I pity anyone that Buba decides to beat up. I remember him now. He is in the next classroom with the older boys and girls."

"Umm," Daniya paused as they reached the outskirts of the village. "It looks as it we have a hard job ahead of us in this village, Deeja. We'll have to pray a lot, won't we?"

"Yes, but remember," Deeja began to sing softly,

"Jesus, Jesus You are our Captain
You will give us victory in the fight."

Daniya joined in the song as they raced the last few yards into their father's compound.

The next day some of the school children seemed a little more friendly. At recess Daniya kept a sharp lookout for Buba but he didn't see him. 'Perhaps Buba's absence explains why the children are more friendly,' Daniya thought.

After school he saw Toma walk off by himself. Daniya hurried after him. "Toma," he began, "how about coming to Sunday School with me on Sunday?"

Toma hesitated. "I don't know . . . it depends . . ."

"Do come," Daniya coaxed. "My father is going to tell the story of a brave man who stayed in a den of lions all night. He will tell us how we can become brave too."

"How?" Toma was interested.

"By letting Jesus come into our hearts," Daniya explained. "Jesus will forgive our sins and sweep our hearts clean from all fear."

Toma's small round face was eager. He drew a deep breath. "I'd sure like that, not to be afraid of Bu ... of anybody any more," he finished hastily. "I'll try and come. Goodbye."

That night, after supper, when the family had gathered around the flickering kerosene lantern for their devotions, Daniya told them about his talk with Toma. After they had read a chapter from the Bible they all prayed earnestly for the people of Dadin-Wanda-Ya-Je. They prayed especially for Toma that God would give him the courage to come to Sunday School.

On Sunday afternoon Daniya waited outside the church door. One or two older people and a few small children drifted shyly into the church. This wasn't a nice long building like the one in their former home in the Village-of-the-Hill-of-Wealth. It was only a small round hut with a thatched roof. But it was swept as neat and clean as Deeja's new grass broom could sweep it. At the front their father had placed a high wooden box for a pulpit. Their mother had covered it with a pretty flowered cloth.

"It looks nice, doesn't it?" Deeja paused a moment beside Daniya, before slipping in and sitting on one of the grass mats near the front.

Just then, Pastor Bako came to the door. "Beat the second gong, my son."

Daniya's heart sank. It was time to begin and Toma had not come. He took up an iron rod and began to beat the larger piece of iron hanging from the mango tree. Bong! Bong! Bong! "Dear Jesus help Toma to come," Daniya

14

prayed. Bong! Bong! Bong! "Help him to come soon," he added as he gave a final loud BONG! and hung up the rod.

But as Daniya entered the church his face broke into a broad smile. Toma was sitting just inside the door. 'He must have slipped in while I was beating the gong,' Daniya thought. He sat down beside Toma and whispered, "Welcome!"

Toma grinned. Then he settled back and listened intently to the story of Daniel. When the story was finished Mrs. Bako stood up. In her hand she held a dirty calabash bowl. "See," she said, "this calabash has fine markings on the outside. But the inside is full of uncleanness. That is what sin does to our hearts——it makes them unclean. Jesus is the only one who can wash away the dirt of sin. It we ask Him, Jesus will forgive all our sins and make our hearts as white as cotton fluff."

There was a wistful look on Toma's face as the boys left the church. "Did you like the words from God's Book?" Daniya asked.

"Yes, they made my heart feel pleasant while I listened." Toma looked up and down the path, then lowered his voice. "But my heart still feels fear."

"It's Buba, isn't it?" Daniya asked.

"Yes, but that's not all — it's . . ."

"I know," Daniya broke in. "You're afraid of the secret in the forest hut. You needn't be though because . . ." he stopped abruptly. There was no one listening. Toma had fled!

Disappointment

2

IN THE DAYS THAT FOLLOWED THE twins tried hard to win the friendship of the school children. But it seemed that only the very young ones were friendly and unafraid.

Binta's elfin face and mischievous ways held a great attraction for the more sturdy Deeja. As Binta skipped and danced her way through the games on the playground Deeja tried to make friends with her but without success.

"I wish I knew what to do to make Binta like me," Deeja pondered as she walked toward home one afternoon. Suddenly her thoughts were interrupted by a child's cry. "No, no, you bad boy. Go away!"

Deeja raced round the bend in the path. A little girl was struggling to protect here calabash of bean cakes from a tall boy.

"Buba," Deeja cried indignantly. "What are you doing?"

Buba turned sharply. "I'm doing what I please, Useless-One. And I please to have a bean cake." He grabbed at the calabash again, but the little girl backed away.

"No, no," she screamed. "My mother has filled an order. They are all counted. You cannot have them."

Deeja pushed into the fray. "If you take even one of her cakes, Buba, I shall go with her to the chief and report you."

Buba hesitated. "The chief wouldn't believe a Useless-One," he sneered.

"That's where you're wrong," Deeja declared. "Your chief knows very well that the followers of Jesus do not tell lies."

Again Buba hesitated. He had no desire to be called before old chief Audu. He had been there too often lately. Would this useless-one really go to the chief? Yes, something in her face made him believe her. But to be out-witted by a girl! His face twisted with anger.

"Go and tell the chief then!" he yelled. He gave the child a violent push knocking the calabash from her hands. "Have fun," he mocked as he loped off.

"Aiya! Aiya!" the child sobbed as she began to pick up the bean cakes. "They'll all be spoiled."

"Never mind," Deeja soothed. "You bring them to me and I'll brush them off and count them as I put them back into your calabash."

They worked busily for a few minutes. "What's your name?" Deeja asked.

"Maryamu," the girl answered, as she wiped her tears away with a sticky hand.

"Well, Maryamu, you have two dozen bean cakes all safe and sound. Is that the right number?"

"Yes." Maryamu's face beamed. "Thank you many, many times." With a quick wave of her hand she lifted the calabash to her head and ran off down the road.

After school the next day Deeja was surprised to find Binta waiting for her under the silk-cotton tree near the edge of the school yard. "Where are the other girls?" Deeja asked.

"Oh, I told them to go on as I had something to tell

17

you," Binta answered carelessly. "I want to thank you for helping my little sister last night."

Deeja gasped. "Is Maryamu your sister?"

"Yes, of course," Binta said. "Didn't you know?"

"No, you see——we——I tried to get to know you but ——you——" Deeja stammered.

"I know," Binta lowered her voice. "I was scared to be seen talking to you. Then Maryamu came home and told us how you stood up to Buba and helped her pick up her bean cakes. So I've decided to be your friend . . . at least when Buba isn't around," she finished with a grin.

"Oh, I'm so glad." Deeja gave a little skip of delight. "And will you come to church with me on Sunday, Binta? Please do," she pleaded.

Binta looked over her shoulder. "Sh—not so loud. Toma told me about the pleasant words he heard last Sunday. I would like to come but I don't know . . ." she hesitated, unhappily.

"Don't worry," Deeja comforted. "I'm so pleased we are friends at last. I'll pray some more about your coming to church. I know God will show us a way."

A few minutes later Deeja bounced into the grinding hut where her mother was grinding guinea corn for their supper. "There is news, Mother," she said. "Binta has promised to be my friend. It's all because I helped Maryamu yesterday. Maryamu is Binta's sister." Deeja's words tumbled over each other in her excitement.

"Madalla! That is splendid," her mother answered. "Now run and find your brother. I have a plan to discuss with you both."

Deeja skipped out to the door of the entrance hut. She

stood poised on one leg for a minute trying to decide in which direction to go to find her brother. Sometimes he visited the dye pits near the edge of the village. It was fascinating to watch the men dip the long pieces of woven cloth into the shallow holes filled with dye; then to watch them pull the cloth out again an entirely different colour. 'I'll go there first,' Deeja thought.

She gave a big hop and started off in the direction of the dye pits. On her way she passed the little mud church. How lonely it looked in the shade of the tall mango tree. "Never mind, little church," Deeja whispered, "it will soon be Sunday. Then we'll come and sing the happy songs again. And perhaps my friend Binta will come too," her dark eyes glowed at the thought.

When she reached the market square she stopped and looked around. The empty stalls were very dirty. Bits of paper and rags littered the ground. Dried pieces of sugar cane and yam peelings were scattered everywhere. "Truly that place needs many hands and many brooms," Deeja thought as she trotted on.

"Deeja! Deeja!"

Deeja turned quickly. Daniya and Toma were coming down a bush path that joined the market road. They were carrying a large stalk of bananas. "Where are you going?" Daniya called.

"I was looking for you," Deeja panted as she ran over to them. "Where have you been?"

"To the farm," Toma answered. "Daniya offered to help me cut this stalk of bananas for my father. Isn't it a splendid big one?"

"Beyond doubt." Deeja admired the fat green bananas hungrily. "They'll soon be ripe, won't they?"

"Yes, when market day returns again, they'll be ready." Toma grinned with satisfaction.

"What did you want me for?" Daniya asked as they all continued on their way towards home.

"Mother said to call you as she has a plan to tell us," Deeja answered.

When they reached the twins' home the boys lowered the stalk of bananas to the floor in the entrance hut. Then they hurried after Deeja into the kitchen.

"See, Mother, we have come," Deeja said. "We are all ready. Do tell us your plan quickly."

"What's it about?" Daniya's face was like a big question mark.

Their mother laughed as she lifted a tray of spinach greens to her lap. With swift deft fingers she began to strip the leaves from their stems. "Well," she said, "how would you like to start a Bible club for all the girls and boys?"

Deeja clapped her hands. "Oh, Mother, what a good idea! Let's do it, Daniya."

Daniya's face clouded. "But, Mother, the kids don't come to Sunday School, so how could we get them to come to the church for a Bible club?"

His mother turned to Toma. "Perhaps you could help, Toma. Do you think the children would be more likely to come to our house than to the church?"

Toma looked thoughtfully from one to the other. "Yes, I think so," he said at last. "Buba didn't say anything about us coming to your house. He just told us we were not to go to the church or follow the 'Jesus Way'. He said your road was full of lies, but Binta and I don't think so. We would like to know more only . . ."

"Fear still catches at your heart," Daniya finished for him.

Toma nodded. "Truly we have much fear when Buba is around," He shifted his position uneasily, then continued. "If we could keep Buba from finding out about the gathering I'm sure the children would come with joy."

"I'll ask Binta to help me spread the word among the girls," Deeja said, jumping up. "Let's just say there will be a nice surprise for them if they come here."

"Could we have it on Friday after school, Mother?" Daniya asked.

"Yes, I think so," she answered. "We will talk it over with your father tonight. Then we will prepare an interesting programme."

As the week advanced, excitement mounted high. Deeja chuckled to herself as one after another of the girls gave her a shy smile, then looked away quickly. "They do want to be friends after all," she thought in relief. "It's only their fear of Buba that has held them back."

Buba seemed aware of something going on. He was always popping out from behind a building or round a corner.

"I wish Buba would stop shadowing me," Daniya grumbled as he and Deeja met Toma after school one day. "He watches me like a monkey does a cornfield. I've hardly had a chance to tell any of the boys about our gathering."

Toma's eyes danced. "Don't worry," he said. "While Buba was following you I was able to tell all the boys." His face suddenly sobered. "I'd sure hate him to catch me being friends with you, though. His uncle is the witch-doctor, you know, and he has much power in our village."

"I know," Daniya said. "But Jesus is more powerful than the witch doctor. I wish you would trust in Him, Toma."

Toma only shook his head so Daniya said no more.

As soon as the dismissal bell rang on Friday afternoon, the twins picked up their study books and raced for home. They wanted to spread some grass mats for the children to sit on in the shade of the compound wall. Toma and Binta had promised to wait at the corner and bring the boys and girls.

"Just in time," Daniya panted as the last mat was put in place. "I hear them coming. Let's go and meet them."

They dashed out towards the road, then stopped in bewilderment. The crowd of boys and girls were scattering in every direction. In another minute there wasn't one to be seen.

Deeja fought back her tears. "Whatever happened to them, Daniya? Did we frighten them?"

"Of course not," Daniya answered. "They hadn't even seen us yet. But without doubt something scared them. I wonder where Toma and Binta are?"

"Pst! pst!" The twins looked towards a high rock at the side of the road. From behind it came a loud whispered, "Daniya! Deeja!"

The twins ran to the rock. Toma and Binta were crouched behind it. Their faces were streaked with tears.

Binta spoke first. "It was Buba who scared the kids away. He beat Toma with great strength," she sobbed.

"Where was he?" Daniya demanded.

"He jumped on me from behind that baobob tree yonder." Toma pointed with his chin toward an old tree standing close to the pathway. "He began to hit me. And

22

he yelled at the other kids that he'd do the same to them too. That's why they all ran home. But the thing that scared us most of all was his awful threat."

"What threat?" Daniya asked quickly.

Binta looked around fearfully. "Tell them, Toma," she said.

Toma leaned close to the twins. His eyes were dark pools of fear and his voice shook as he whispered, "He said that—that anyone who came to your house or the church would have the curse of the forest hut upon them."

The twins sat very still. Neither spoke as they stared at each other in shocked dismay.

Along the Forest Trail

3 "AIYA!" DEEJA SIGHED. "THE CHILDREN will be afraid now and won't come again."

"Yes," Daniya agreed, discouragement sweeping over him. "Even though we know Buba's words are full of foolishness and the curse cannot harm them, *they* do not know it. And the fear of it will catch them and keep them away from us."

Toma sat up. "Do you mean there is no power in a curse from the forest hut?"

"Yes, that's just what I mean," Daniya answered. "God tells us all about it in His Book in Psalm 115. The eyes in an idol cannot see. Their mouths cannot talk. Their feet cannot walk. Whatever idols or other things they have in the forest hut they are all made by some man. They have no life in them so how could they harm anyone?"

"And," Deeja added, "in that same chapter God also says, 'They that make them are like unto them; so is every one that trusteth in them'."

Toma looked uncertainly from one twin to the other. "But I trust in them, and I can walk and talk and see just as well as you can."

Daniya smiled. "It's the eyes of your heart that are blind, Toma. I'll prove it to you if you show me where the forest hut is."

Binta leaned back against the rock. A thoughtful frown puckered her forehead as she stared at her older brother. Toma squirmed unhappily. Suddenly he set his chin in a determined line. "All right. I'll take you tomorrow night. Our father showed me where the hut was when I was with him in the forest one day. He helps the witch-doctor, you know."

"Is your father's name Ali Mele?" Daniya asked.

"Yes," Toma answered. "He has gone away for a couple of days though, so I don't think there will be anyone at the hut tomorrow night. I'll take you as far as the clearing, but that's all."

"Good!" Daniya jumped up. "Let's go and tell mother why the kids all ran away. She will be wondering what has happened to us."

"Binta and I won't come any further today," Toma said. "Buba may still be lurking around. But I'll meet you at the tall palm tree behind your home tomorrow night, Daniya."

Daniya nodded. Then he and Deeja raced towards home and were soon pouring out the whole story into the sympathetic ears of their mother. She clicked her tongue in amazement when she heard how Buba had frightened the children with his threat. "He's a bad one that boy," she said finally. "It will take a 'whatsoever verse' to bring him into the fold of the Good Shepherd."

"And whatsoever ye shall ask in my name, that will I do, that the Father may be glorified in the Son." Daniya repeated the words from John 14. 13 softly.

"I like the one in John 15.16. But I don't know it all. Shall I read it, Mother?" Deeja asked.

Her mother placed a pot of water on the fireplace made

from three stones set close together. She poked the fire to a blaze then she said, "Yes, daughter. Read it and then we shall pray for Buba and ask Jesus to save him."

Deeja read slowly, "Ye have not chosen me, but I have chosen you, and ordained you, that ye should go and bring forth fruit, and that your fruit should remain: that whatsoever ye shall ask of the Father in my name, He may give it you."

For the rest of the day the twins were very quiet. It was hard to get over their keen disappointment in the failure of their Bible club. Daniya wondered if Toma would be brave enough to keep his promise. He also wondered just how he was going to prove to Toma that their spirit worship was useless. It was one thing to be sure in his own heart, but quite another thing to be able to prove his words to someone else. "God will show me a way," Daniya comforted himself.

Deeja wandered around aimlessly. Daniya knew she wanted to go with him to the forest hut. However he thought it would be better if just Toma and he went this time. After all, the witch doctor might be there and they would have to run for it. Of course Deeja could run as fast as he could — if not faster! Still, the forest at night just wasn't a place for girls, he concluded.

The following night the moon was hidden behind a bank of clouds. The two boys peered anxiously into the gloom as they stumbled along the forest trail. Daniya was praying in his heart, "Help me, Lord Jesus, and show me what to do so I can lead Toma into your path."

"What's that?" Abruptly Toma clutched Daniya's arm.

"Sh — " Daniya whispered. "I think there is someone

following us." The boys held their breath. Sure enough there was a soft pit-pat of bare feet coming down the trail behind them.

"Let's crouch down here and see who it is," Daniya said. He could feel Toma trembling as he dropped down beside him. Daniya watched from his hiding-place. The moon peeped fitfully from behind a cloud. Suddenly Daniya chuckled. "It's the girls, Deeja and Binta. They have followed us."

With a grunt of disgust Toma sprang to his feet. "What do you girls think you're doing?" he demanded.

"Oh!" Binta gasped and clung to Deeja for a moment.

Deeja began to giggle. "At least we're not hiding in the grass and jumping out at people," she teased. "Come on, we want to be in on this too."

Toma turned to Daniya. "Shall we chase them home?"

"No." Daniya sighed. "Since they've come this far they may as well go with us. But no screaming, remember," he ordered, as he started off after Toma once again.

"As if we would," Deeja spluttered, falling into line behind the boys and Binta.

Soon they came to a fork in the trail. Toma turned to the right and led the way down a very narrow path. Tall grass waved higher than their heads on either side. The trees grew straight and crowded, close together. A heavy oppressive silence hovered over the forest.

Toma was a little way ahead. Suddenly he gave a sharp cry, "Aiya! a snake has bitten me. Help, quick!"

Daniya dashed forward just in time to see the tail of the snake disappear into the grass. "Quick, Toma. Sit down and show me just where it bit you," Daniya urged.

"My father has taught me how to cut a snake wound and make it bleed. We must do it at once."

"Can you see it?" Toma asked anxiously, as he sat down and felt around the sore spot on his foot.

Daniya bent close and strained his eyes. Just then the moon shook off the last gloomy cloud and beamed down upon them in all its brilliance. "Yawa!" Daniya exclaimed. "Now I can see it clearly. That is indeed a thing of thanks to God."

"Shouldn't we tie it first? Father said . . ." Deeja began.

"Yes, hurry. Tie your headscarf here on his ankle. Tie it tightly so the poison won't go up his leg," Daniya said. Then with his knife he made several cuts over the fang marks on Toma's foot, making it bleed freely.

"Was it an evil snake, the owner-of-death kind?" Binta shivered, as she asked the question.

"I don't know," Daniya answered. "Did you see what kind it was, Toma?"

"No. I — I — couldn't see it well enough," Toma's voice trembled. "I think it was sort of brown and only about two feet long."

Daniya said quickly, "Never mind, Toma. Do not be afraid. We will take you to my father and he will tell us what to do."

"And we will all pray hard," Deeja added. "God is the greatest Doctor of all, you know. I'm sure He will make you well again."

"Let's go with haste then," Toma begged. "Our oldest brother died from a snake bite. But I don't want to die yet. I'm not ready to die," he whispered fearfully, "I'm not ready at all."

Toma was of a slighter build than Daniya, and with a little effort he was hoisted up on Daniya's back and they started towards home. The bright moonlight cast dancing shadows ahead of them as they hurried down the trail. Every few minutes they stopped and loosened the bandage around Toma's ankle. Then they tightened it and pressed on.

When they reached the fork in the road and turned into the wider trail the two girls clasped hands and carried Toma between them for awhile until Daniya was rested. It seemed a long time to the weary children, but at last they reached the village and the girls ran ahead to tell Pastor Bako what had happened.

He immediately prepared a fire in Daniya's room and when Toma was lowered onto the mat near the fire Pastor Bako examined the foot closely. "You have done well, my son," he said to Daniya. "See, the swelling is but slight. We will remove the bandage now and wash the wound with some disinfectant." He worked quickly as he spoke.

Mrs. Bako covered Toma with a blanket and gave him a drink of warm gruel. Then they all gathered round him and prayed earnestly that God would make him well again.

"Deeja," her mother said presently, "you slip home with Binta and tell their mother about Toma. She will want to come over and see him."

It was a long and difficult night. Toma was restless with pain and his low moans kept his mother and Binta in constant fear. Finally Daniya slipped in and sat down on the mat beside Toma. "Toma," he whispered, "is it the pain that keeps you awake?"

"Yes, but that's not all," Toma hugged the blanket to him and shuddered violently. "I keep thinking that the spirits of the forest hut sent the snake to bite me because they didn't want us to go to their hut. And now perhaps they will come and snatch me away like they did my big brother."

"No, Toma, you must not think that, because it isn't so. If you would only ask Jesus to come into your heart He would sweep away all your fears and make your heart lie down in peace."

"Oh, I would like to do that," Toma's voice was filled with longing. "But how can I go to church tomorrow with my sore foot?"

"You don't have to wait until you go to church," Daniya assured him. "Jesus is waiting here right now and if you ask Him to come into your heart He will do so."

Sudden hope sprang up in Toma's eyes. He raised himself on one elbow as he asked, "Do you mean that, Daniya?"

"Of course." Daniya smiled. "Just close your eyes and tell Jesus you want Him to come into your heart and wash it clean."

Toma wasted no more time but promptly shut his eyes. "Oh, Jesus," he began, "please come into my heart and sweep out all the badness. Take away my fear of the spirits of the forest hut and help me to follow Your way of joy. And if You agree, please make my foot better again. Thank You very much." Toma's voice was a little shaky, but when he opened his eyes they were shining with an inner radiance. "Jesus heard me, didn't He?" he said.

Daniya nodded. "Yes, Toma. Jesus always hears those who call upon Him in truth."

The firelight danced on the bamboo rafters and flickered over Binta's face as she lay curled up in a corner — asleep at last. It rested for a moment on the weary form of her mother as she sat huddled against the wall, then it shone softly into Toma's glowing eyes. Daniya looked at his friend. A great wave of thankfulness swept over him and filled his heart with gladness. Toma, his pal Toma, was now walking with him in the 'Jesus Way'!

The Twins Try Again

4 THE NEXT DAY TOMA'S FOOT WAS STILL painful, but the swelling was down. When Pastor Bako looked at it, he said, "God has answered our prayers for you, my son. I feel sure now that your foot will soon be well again."

Toma's mother had been watching anxiously. Now the worried lines in her face relaxed. She fell down in front of Pastor Bako, and clapping her hands together, she thanked him over and over again.

"It is the Lord Jesus who has heard our cry and who is making your son well again," Pastor Bako explained. "You must thank Him."

But Mrs. Ali Mele only shook her head. "I do not understand the 'Jesus Words'," she said.

"I do," Toma broke in. "Jesus came into my heart last night and swept it white and clean."

Binta was disappointed. "Oh, Toma! I didn't see Him. Did He come when I was sleeping?" she asked.

"Yes, you were sleeping. I didn't see Him with these eyes in my head, you know. But the eyes in my heart saw Him and I know that He is here." Toma placed his hand over his heart as he spoke.

Deeja looked at Binta's puzzled face. "Ask your mother if you can come with me to Sunday School," she whispered. "Then perhaps the 'Jesus Words' will come clear in your head."

Binta looked doubtful, and when the twins went out into the kitchen she followed them. "What about Buba?" she asked. "If he saw me going to church he would tell his uncle. Then perhaps the curse of the forest hut would catch me."

"He also told you not to come to our house and you've been here all night without anything catching you," Deeja reasoned. "Don't worry, Binta. We will watch out for Buba. If we see him you can hide in the grass until he is out of sight."

"And when you come to Jesus, He will sit in your heart and chase away all those fears," Daniya assured her.

Binta's mother only shrugged her shoulders when she heard her daughter's request. Binta took this as consent, and ran off home to get ready.

Daniya stayed with Toma and the two boys spent a happy morning together. Daniya read one story after another from his Bible. Toma listened eagerly. His mother dozed in the shade of the entrance hut. After awhile she got up and told the boys that she would go home and prepare food for her family but would return later.

Toma watched her leave. Then he said, "Do you think my parents will every understand about Jesus and let Him live in their hearts, Daniya?"

"Yes, I'm sure they will if we all pray for them," Daniya answered, turning in his Bible to the sixteenth chapter of Acts. "Shall I read you the story of a jailor and his family who all became 'Jesus followers' at the same time? Guess if a tough man like a jailor could follow Jesus, your father and mother can too."

"Read it," Toma ordered as he lay back on his mat once more.

When the others returned from church Daniya looked at his twin as he nodded slightly in Binta's direction. Deeja shook her head, so he knew that Binta had not given her heart to Jesus yet.

Early the following morning Pastor Bako heard someone call a greeting from the door of the entrance hut. It was Ali Mele. He had just arrived home, and had hurried over as soon as his wife told him the news about Toma. He was a tall thin man with long tribal marks down each cheek. A dark grey blanket was thrown loosely over his shoulders. His eyes were wary as he stepped into the pastor's compound.

"Greetings of the day, Ali Mele," Pastor Bako said. "Did you return well?"

"Well," answered Ali Mele. Then they both went through a set of prolonged greetings as they inquired politely concerning the health of each other's household.

Finally Pastor Bako led Ali Mele into the hut where Toma was. Toma sat up and rubbed the sleep from his eyes. "You have come, Father," he said.

His father greeted him and bent to examine the sore foot. Then he stood up and turned to Pastor Bako. "Thank you for your help. I will take my son home now and give him medicine of strength from the forest hut."

"No, Father," Toma protested. "Please let me stay here. I don't want to take the witch doctor's medicine."

"Let your son stay with us for a few more days," Pastor Bako suggested. "I believe that God has heard our prayers for him, but he needs careful treatment and much quietness for the next few days. It is not good for him to be moved."

Ali Mele was reluctant, but at last he agreed to leave Toma there until he had consulted with the witchdoctor. The following evening he returned and said that Toma must go home at once.

"All right, Father," Toma said. "But I cannot take the medicine from the forest hut because I am a 'Jesus follower' now."

Ali Mele drew his brows together in a dark frown. "We'll see about that," was all he said as he lifted Toma to his back and left the compound.

The next day the twins waited for Binta along the road. They all crouched down in the long grass and the twins listened breathlessly as Binta told them her news. "Father tried to make Toma drink the medicine from the witchdoctor," she began, "but Toma closed his mouth with much strength and kept shaking his head. Then father took off the clean bandage and rubbed some slimy black stuff on Toma's foot. Yet would you believe it!" Binta's eyes were filled with wonder. "This morning, when I went in to greet Toma, the slimy medicine was all gone and the white bandage was back on his foot!"

"Yawa! Good for Toma," Daniya exclaimed. "I am glad he was brave enough to refuse the medicine of darkness."

"I don't think I could be that brave," Binta said. "I am sure our father will whip Toma when he discovers the white bandages on his foot again."

"It is Jesus who is helping Toma to be brave," Deeja said. "He would give you a strong heart, too, if you would trust in Him."

When the twins told Pastor Bako about Toma, he went at once to see him, taking Daniya with him. They found

Ali Mele in the entrance hut. He was looking gloomy and upset. After the usual greetings they asked to see Toma.

When Ali Mele hesitated, Pastor Bako said, "I have brought fresh bandages and medicine for your son. I know you want to use your medicine, but it is not good to mix the medicine of darkness with the medicine of light. Will you not let us try our treatment for a few days longer?"

Without a word Ali Mele rose to his feet and led the way to Toma's sleeping hut. At the door he stopped. "My son tells me that he is following your 'Jesus Way' now. He has refused the way of our fathers. Do with him as you like, but if he dies — we will chase you from our village."

"He will not die," Pastor Bako said calmly, as he and Daniya entered the hut.

Toma smiled when he saw them. "I heard what my father said, yet it does not frighten me," he told them. "Is not that a thing of wonder?"

"See! you have become brave like Daniel," said Daniya, grinning at him.

For the rest of the week Pastor Bako went daily to care for Toma and to make sure that his instructions were being carried out. Toma's foot healed rapidly and near the end of the next week he was back in school.

The boys gave up their plan of going to the forest hut for the present at least. "It really isn't necessary now as far as you're concerned," Daniya said. "God showed you in His own way that His road is the best one."

"Yes," Toma agreed. "I know now that God's power is greater than that of the forest hut. He has chased away all my fears and He made my heart strong even when father was angry with me."

36

The twins, as well as Toma and Binta, were all for having another Bible club meeting on Friday. The four sat behind the big rock near the old baobob tree and discussed plans. But they always ended at the same problem — how to overcome the children's fear of coming to the twins' home.

Suddenly Toma jumped to his feet. "I've got it! Let's have the Bible club at our house."

"Father won't . . ." Binta began doubtfully.

"I heard father say that tomorrow he is going to take some guinea corn to sell at the big market beyond the hills. He won't be back until darkness falls," Toma said. "Our mother won't care what we do. Would your mother come and teach the lesson at our house, Daniya?"

"Yes, I'm sure she would if your mother agrees. And since Buba hasn't threatened the kids about going to your house, perhaps they would go there tomorrow," Daniya answered.

"Have you told any of the kids that you are following the 'Jesus Way' now?" Deeja asked Toma.

Toma shook his head. "Not yet," he said. "I thought I could tell them all together at the Bible club."

"That's a splendid idea, Toma," Daniya said, delighted. "Let's go and tell mother now."

Mrs. Bako agreed heartily to the new plan. Pastor Bako showed Daniya how to give an object lesson with some hemp strands. First he tied Daniya's hands together with a thin strand which Daniya was able to break at once. Then he wound a long piece of the rope around Daniya's hands and arms and around his whole body a number of times. Finally Daniya realized he couldn't break loose without his father's help.

As his father took his knife and cut Daniya loose, he said, "Thus it is with sin, my son. You begin with small things from which you feel you can break loose at any time. But if you continue, Satan will have you in his power. As this knife set you free, even so faith in Jesus Christ alone can set us free from sin and Satan."

This time the children were more successful in keeping the news of the Bible club from Buba. By four o'clock on Friday afternoon the large compound was packed with boys and girls. Deeja taught them her favourite chorus.

Jesus, Jesus You are our Captain
You will give us victory in the fight
The power of Satan will fall down
Because our Lord is the owner of victory.

The children shouted with laughter when Daniya tied Toma up with the long hemp rope. But they all clicked their tongues in agreement when the lesson was explained to them. They listened closely as Toma told about the snake bite and how God had answered his prayer in making him well again. "And," he concluded, "just like Daniya's knife cut me free from the rope, so Jesus has washed my heart clean and set me free from all my fears."

Mrs. Bako didn't talk very long. But when she asked who would like to have a clean heart, Binta jumped up and said, "I would."

After the other children had left, Dauda and Hassen, two eleven year old boys and friends of Toma, stayed behind. They also accepted Jesus as their Saviour.

That evening the twins were jubilant. Their mother had a difficult time getting them settled down for the night.

"I'm so glad we came to this town of Happiness-for-all-who-go-there," Deeja yawned as she unbuckled her sandals. "Binta is the nicest friend I've ever had. And to think she now belongs to Jesus too!"

"Of course there's still Buba," Daniya paused on his way to his room. "But we have the 'whatsoever verses' for him so it will be all right."

The following week the teacher made an announcement that set the whole school buzzing. He told them that he wanted to see how they were obeying his lessons on the care of animals. In two weeks time they were all to bring their pets to school. A prize would be given to the owner of the most healthy animal.

As soon as school was out Deeja and Daniya's feet fairly skimmed over the dusty pathway towards home.

"I've got to go down to the stream. I want to get some of that nice tender grass for Garba," Daniya panted.

Deeja pulled off her headscarf and wiped her perspiring face as she ran.' 'Oh you needn't worry about your Golden Garba. He is the healthiest, friendliest goat in the whole world. And he's such a lovely golden brown colour too."

Daniya grinned as he ducked under the low doorway into the entrance hut and picked up his scythe. "You speak words of truth, my sister," he said. "Nevertheless, instead of river grass every second day, Oh Garba, from now on you shall eat of the tender grass every day."

The children ran over to the goat hut and opened the door. Garba came prancing out and frisked around them in delight. Suddenly Deeja pounced on a big red rooster that was strutting around the yard. Picking him up in her arms she examined him carefully.

"Daniya, do you think my old Zakara here will win a prize?" she asked hopefully.

Daniya looked the rooster over critically. "I don't

see why not. He is the owner of much fatness. But Deeja . . ." Daniya stopped abruptly.

"But what?" Deeja asked.

"Didn't you promise Zakara for the special offering? That offering is to be taken next Sunday. Zakara will be gone by the day of the contest."

Deeja nodded dumbly. Slowly two big tears slid down her brown cheeks. She had forgotten about her promise for the special offering. Would it matter if she broke her promise just this once? Should she? *Could* she?

The Missing Goat

5 DURING THE NEXT FEW DAYS DEEJA WAS very quiet. When the other girls asked her what pet she was preparing for the contest she told them about Zakara — the biggest, nicest rooster in the district. Well he *was* still hers, wasn't he? she argued to herself.

Then a brilliant plan popped into her mind. She would keep Zakara until the next special offering day. There would be another one at Christmas time. Surely a few more months wouldn't matter as long as she kept her promise in the end. Deeja went off to find her father and tell him of her plan.

Pastor Bako's eyes were kind as he looked at his little daughter. Opening his Bible he began to read from 2 Corinthians 9. 7. "Every man according as he purposeth in his heart, so let him give; not grudgingly, or of necessity: for God loveth a cheerful giver." He gave Deeja the Bible as he said, "I want you to learn that verse, Deeja, and then do whatever God tells you to do."

The Sunday of the special offering dawned bright and clear. A playful breeze, fragrant with a mixture of moist earth and growing things, swept round the corner of the chicken hut. It whipped the tattered mat hanging over the doorway into Deeja's face as she peered into the hut. "Come here, Zakara," she called. The big rooster came forward at once and ate greedily from her hand. Deeja tied

41

a stout string around his foot and fastened him securely. Then she took a rough gourd sponge and brushed his feathers until they gleamed.

"Now you be good and stay nice and clean until I am ready for you," she warned him cheerfully. "You are a very fortunate rooster because you are chosen as a special gift offering." Zakara preened himself and crowed loudly. "Kaiya!" Deeja giggled. "You shouldn't act so proud. But I must admit you do look nice."

She ran back to her room and put on her Sunday dress and headscarf. As she picked up Zakara and joined the rest of the family on their way to church, Deeja's heart was singing. Her mother was carrying the three large water pots she had made for her special offering. 'How beautiful mother looks in her blue Sunday cloth,' Deeja thought, 'and what a peaceful and contented face she has.'

Daniya shifted his bundle of short hoe handles on his shoulder and grinned at Deeja. It had been a lot of work cutting the wood and whittling the handles to just the right size and shape. But he was glad now that he had kept at it. "The Lord deserves our very best," their father had told them.

The twins knew their father carried some of his best guinea corn in the large bag which he placed near the pulpit when they reached the church. They were early, but blind Haruna was already sitting patiently just inside the door. Four ears of corn tied in a small bundle lay beside him.

"Even poor blind Haruna has brought a gift," Deeja whispered to Daniya, as she tied Zakara to his hoe handles. "I'm so glad Jesus helped me to give Zakara. It

42

would be terrible not to give Him anything when He gives us so much every day."

Soon an older man and three women arrived. Then a group of small children slipped in. Their bright eyes opened wide as they saw the gifts at the front of the church. Staring and giggling they pushed and tumbled over each other as they crowded close together on the grass mats.

"None of those children attend school," Daniya muttered, as Deeja opened the hymn book they shared. "They likely haven't heard Buba's threat yet and that is why they are not afraid to come."

Just then there was a commotion at the door and all heads were turned in that direction. Binta and Toma hurried in. They were each carrying a pigeon. Behind them came Hassen and Dauda with two cornstalk cages.

Pastor Bako's eyes twinkled. "Are these cages for the pigeons?" he asked.

"Yes," Toma answered. "Hassen and Dauda didn't have much time to get an offering ready. They have not been Christians very long, you know. So we said they could make the cages for our pigeons."

Dauda and Hassen were a bit anxious as they held out their offerings. "Are they all right?" Dauda asked.

"This is how you open the door on my cage," Hassen demonstrated eagerly.

"They are just splendid," Pastor Bako told them. He took the cages and placed them near the wall. Then he said, "Toma and Binta, perhaps you had better put the pigeons in their cages now and we will begin the service. You have all done well and I'm sure God is pleased. When we sell these things the money will be sent to the evangelist and his wife in the village of Tall Forest. Theirs is a village where much darkness sits in the hearts of the people. They need our help."

Near the end of the service the twins were startled to see Yakubu, a pal of Buba's, enter the church and sit down close to the door. What did it mean? Had Yakubu come to spy and would Buba be waiting along the path to pounce on the four who had dared go against his threat? They saw Dauda and Hassen glance quickly at Toma. But Toma only shook his head and smiled, so the boys relaxed and turned their attention back to the message.

"How brave Toma has become, now that he is a 'Jesus follower'," Daniya thought. "And Binta too!" She had only given Yakubu a hasty glance before turning her eyes back again to Pastor Bako's face.

As soon as they were dismissed Deeja said, "Let's all walk home together, then Buba can't do much even if . . ."

"Sh-h-h-h-here comes Yakubu," Daniya warned as Yakubu sauntered towards them. He was a short thickset boy of about thirteen. He eyed the little group doubtfully as he said, "Did you really give all those hoe handles and pigeons and things away *free*?"

"Yes, of course we did," Deeja said.

Yakubu was puzzled. "Why? What's the good of it?"

Daniya realized that Yakuba had missed the explanation in church so he told him all about the special offering. Yakubu seemed impressed. He hesitated for a minute then he blurted out, "But I didn't see a goat there. We — I — I heard you were giving your goat away too."

"Oh no," Daniya answered. "I gave the hoe handles. My goat is still at home. Do you want to see it?"

"I suppose so." Yakubu spoke carelessly, but a sudden gleam of satisfaction shone in his eyes. When he saw

44

Garba he gave a low whistle. "Kai!" he exclaimed. "He certainly is a goat of much health and strength. No wonder . . ."

Toma was curious. "No wonder . . . what?"

Yakubu shrugged. "Oh nothing." He turned back to Daniya and asked, "Do you let your goat loose every day?"

"Yes, I let him run around until it is nearly dark and then I lock him in for the night." Daniya loosed Garba from the goat hut as he spoke.

Yakubu bent over and picked up a piece of grass. "Don't tell me you bring him this river grass every day?"

Daniya laughed. "Yes, I do now since I've been getting him ready for the contest. Garba is a goat of much wisdom, you know. He prefers the river grass to any other kind."

"That's likely because river grass *is* sweeter," Toma said. "It's like me since I entered the 'Jesus Way'. I like His road best now and it *is* the best way too."

"And it is the *only* true way to Heaven," Deeja added.

"Yes," Daniya agreed. He followed Yakubu to the door of the entrance hut and said, "How about coming to church again sometime, Yakubu?"

"Perhaps I might," Yakubu said slowly. "Do you only go on Sunday?"

"Well, there is a little prayer service at six o'clock on Thursday evenings," Daniya said. "Would you like to come to that?"

"Do you all go?" Yakubu asked.

"Yes, we usually do," Daniya told him.

"All right, I'll come and go with you," Yakubu said as he hurried away.

The other children gathered around Daniya and stared

after the retreating figure in open mouthed amazement. Dauda was the first to speak. "I've never seen him so friendly. Never!" he said as he squeezed his thin wiry body past the others and stepping outside, continued to gaze after Yakubu.

"Why was he so interested in your goat?" Binta questioned. "Do you suppose he has a goat for the contest too?"

Daniya shook his head in bewilderment. "No, I heard him tell someone that he had a pig for the contest, so it couldn't be that. But I have a feeling there *is* something queer going on."

The twins walked all the way home with their four friends. They kept a sharp lookout for Buba along the way but he didn't appear.

That evening as Daniya was locking up Garba for the night, he suddenly called, "Deeja, come here. I've got an idea."

Deeja gave a few vigorous stirs to the hot spicy gravy bubbling over the fire. Then wiping the smoke tears from her eyes with one end of her headscarf, she ran out of the kitchen and over to the goat hut. "What is it?" she asked.

"I've just been thinking that we can share Garba. As from now, half of him belongs to you," Daniya said generously.

"Which half? His head or his feet?" Deeja asked with a chuckle. Then she sobered. "Do you really mean it, Daniya?"

"Of course," he answered. "After all, you have often fed him for me. You always help me to find him when he wanders out of bounds. And anyway we are twins and share everything else, don't we?"

46

"Yes," Deeja said, her eyes lighting up with pleasure. "And I'll help you cut river grass for him from now on too. Thank you many many times, Daniya. I do hope he wins a prize."

"So do I," said Daniya, giving Garba a last pat before closing the door.

All the next week the school children could think and talk of only one thing—the animal contest on Friday. The twins had not been able to arrange another Bible club because Toma and Binta's mother said that one was all they could have in their home. And now with the children's minds on the contest, Mrs. Bako thought they had better wait until next week before trying again.

On Thursday the teacher announced, "I'm going to give you a long noon hour tomorrow. But you must all be here with your pets by two o'clock."

Later than afternoon Deeja was surprised to see Daniya take a long rope and tie Garba to the palm tree behind the compound. "Better be safe," he said. "This is one night we don't want Golden Garba to wander away from home."

"Good idea." Deeja took up her Bible and they started for the church. Suddenly she stopped. "Aren't you going to wait for Yakubu or has he changed his mind about coming?"

"He hasn't said anything more about it." Daniya shaded his eyes against the glare of the setting sun and stared back down the road. The next moment his face broke into a glad smile. "Yauwa! Here he comes now."

Yakubu seemed very uncomfortable and didn't say much on the way to church. As soon as the service was over he said a quick goodbye and raced towards home.

"He didn't seem very interested, did he?" said Deeja, disappointed.

"No," Daniya agreed. "I just don't understand him. But let's hurry home now it's getting dark and time Garba was in his hut."

The twins sped down the road, jumped high over the fallen tree stump behind the kitchen and then pulled to a sudden stop under the old palm tree. Part of the rope was still tied to the tree. It had been cut neatly in half and Garba—Golden Garba was gone!

The Broken Promise

6 "STOLEN!" ANNOUNCED DANIYA. "Garba has been stolen!"

"Surely not!" Pastor Bako exclaimed, as he entered the compound. "He must have broken the rope, my son."

"Come and see, Father." Daniya and Deeja excitedly pulled their father toward the palm tree and showed him the rope. Pastor Bako examined it carefully. His face was stern as he straightened up. "Beyond doubt your goat has been stolen. Just leave the rope as it is. I shall go and tell the chief."

Their mother tried to cheer up the twins and persuade them to eat their supper. "Perhaps they let Garba loose in the forest and you can find him in the morning," she suggested.

"But Mother," Deeja sobbed, "there's no time! We have to go to school in the morning and the contest begins at two o'clock."

"A hyena will likely eat him before morning," Daniya said with the calmness of despair. "I heard one crying last night. It sounded quite near."

"God is able to protect your goat in the forest as well as in his own little hut," their mother reminded them.

When their father returned he told them that the chief would send some of his men to the forest in the morning to hunt for the goat. "He is sure it is a prank because of the contest and thinks they'll likely find Garba nearby."

The memory verse for their evening devotions was from Matthew 7. 7 'Ask, and it shall be given you; seek, and ye shall find; knock, and it shall be opened unto you.'

The dismal faces of the twins broke into smiles as they repeated the wonderful promise over and over again. After all it was a long time until two o'clock and God knew where Garba was even if they didn't.

The next morning as they were on their way to school the twins heard a low grunting and snorting in the tall grass by the roadside. "Sounds like a pig," Daniya said, as he parted the grass and peered around. "Yes, here he is. Kai! isn't he a one of great size?"

Deeja gazed at the large friendly pig. "Say do you think he is for the contest, Daniya? Look, there's a piece of rope around his foot."

"Not another stolen animal, I hope," muttered Daniya, making a quick grab at the rope and holding it fast. "No, this looks as if it has been broken. Come on you owner-of-fatness," he commanded, tugging at the rope. "Today it's school for you — at least until your owner arrives."

The twins pulled and pushed and struggled with the reluctant pig. They were hot and breathless by the time they reached the school yard.

Instantly they were surrounded by a noisy crowd of boys and girls. "We found him along the road," Daniya explained. "Does anyone know to whom he belongs?"

"I think it is Yakubu's pig," one boy volunteered.

"Yakubu," Toma called as they saw Yakubu enter the yard, "did you lose your pig?"

"Yes," he yelled, running towards the group. "Have you seen it?"

"The twins found it for you," the children answered, pointing toward the pig and dancing up and down in their excitement.

Yakubu's face lit up with joy but he looked at the twins strangely. "You mean you found it and brought it all this way for me?" he asked.

"Yes, of course," Daniya answered. "We felt sure it was for the contest and we would find its owner here. I only wish someone would find our goat and bring it back. It was stolen last night."

"Stolen!" the children gasped.

"How do you know it didn't break loose like my pig?" Yakubu challenged.

"Because the rope was cut," Daniya answered. "Anyway the chief knows about it and he is sending men out to find it this morning."

"Huh, a lot of good that will do," Buba scoffed. "Those men aren't any good at finding things."

Daniya noticed that Yakubu shot Buba a troubled look. But just then the bell rang and everyone scattered to their classes.

At recess time one of the boys from the next classroom handed Daniya a note. It read: 'Thanks for bringing my pig back. Your goat is in that tiny grass shelter behind the market. Please don't let anyone know I told you because I promised not to tell.'

"Yakubu!" Daniya exclaimed as he showed the note to Deeja. "I see it all now. He only went to church with us to make sure we were out of the way when Buba came to steal our goat. And now that the chief knows about it he is scared."

"Or perhaps he really is trying to repay us for catching

his pig," Deeja said. "But oh, Daniya, nothing matters now as long as we can get Garba back in time for the contest."

"We'll dash over to the market the minute school is out at noon," Daniya assured her. "We'll just have time."

The hands of the clock moved far too slowly for all the children that morning. However, eleven o'clock finally arrived and they were dismissed.

With fast pounding hearts the twins raced towards the market. Falling on their knees in front of the grass shelter they peered into the dimness. Garba looked up from munching some river grass and greeted them with a loud baa.

"To think they even gave you some river grass," Deeja said, giving him a pat of welcome.

"I told Yakubu that Garba liked the river grass, remember?" Daniya said, leading Garba out. "So, of course, they knew he wouldn't be any trouble to bring over here as long as they held river grass in front of him. He looks all right, though he's a bit dirty. Let's hurry so we can clean him up a little."

By two o'clock the excited children were all gathered in the school yard. There was quite a collection of pigs and goats and chickens, as well as a few pigeons, dogs and one sleepy little donkey. The teacher and the chief arrived together. The chief, his long white robes billowing around him, went from one group to the other judging the pets.

The twins saw Buba glowering at them all through the judging. He was showing a young goat that looked rather small and stunted compared to Garba. "I suppose that is one reason why he didn't want us to show ours," Deeja whispered to Daniya.

"Sh-h-h," Daniya hushed her. "Here comes the chief."

"I heard you found your goat," the chief said as he recognized the twins. "No wonder someone wanted him out of the way. He is truly a goat full of health."

Finally all the animals had been inspected and the teacher called for silence. The chief made a short speech. He encouraged the children to continue taking good care of their pets. Then he said, "The first prize goes to Yakubu for his pig. We know the pig was given to him when it was only a small thing full of sickness and it has taken much care to make it into such a pig of fatness."

All the children clapped and cheered as Yakubu was given five shillings. Then the chief called the twins to come forward with Garba. He gave them each two shillings as he said, "This is a very fine goat. He was stolen last night and some of my men wasted all morning hunting for him. This is a serious offence and I think the one who did it should be found and punished."

Daniya glanced at Yakubu's downcast face. Buba was scowling furiously, but there was a scared look in his eyes.

Daniya took a deep breath. Then he said, "Please, Chief, we are happy to have our goat back again. If you agree, we would rather let the words be finished here and nothing more be said about it."

The chief nodded slowly. "All right," he said, turning to the boys and girls. "I agree for this time but if I ever hear of such a thing again I shall not let the words drop so easily."

Later that afternoon as the twins scampered down the

narrow trail towards the river, their tongues kept time to their hurrying feet. They were on their way to find the tenderest, greenest river grass that Garba had ever eaten.

"He really deserves the very best for winning us such a grand prize," Deeja declared, pulling to a stop before a tall clump of green grass."

"One and two!" Daniya gave two great sweeps with his scythe. "Two whole shillings," he sang, "and all my very own. What are you going to do with your money, Deeja?"

"I —" Deeja began, then stopped abruptly as the air was suddenly rent with angry screams and shouts for help.

The twins dropped their scythes and ran toward the bend of the river from which direction the screams were coming. The water was very shallow in the river and the twins slipped down the bank and ran along the dry edge of the wide river bed. As they rounded the bend they saw Yakubu and Buba struggling furiously.

Buba gave Yakubu a heavy blow and knocked him to his knees. "Take that," he screamed, beating him again and again. "You tell-tale! You promised you wouldn't tell. But I know you did, else how would they have found their goat?"

Daniya and Deeja waited no longer but rushed headlong into the battle. They both landed on Buba at once and to his surprise he suddenly found Daniya sitting on his chest and Deeja holding his legs down.

"Promise you'll leave Yakubu alone," Daniya panted.

Admiration flashed for a moment across Buba's face as he looked at the twins. Then he grunted, "And if I don't — what will you two useless-ones do about it?"

Deeja settled herself more comfortably on Buba's legs. "We'll just sit here all night," she declared calmly.

Daniya knew that Buba was stalling for time to get his breath back. And once Buba decided to get up Daniya felt sure that even their combined efforts couldn't hold him down. He spoke quickly. "We know you stole our goat, Buba, and if you don't promise to leave Yakubu alone we'll go to the chief and tell him everything."

At the mention of the chief, Buba's eyes darkened. Then he mocked, "Useless tell-tales all of you!" With a sudden twist he threw off the twins and scrambled to his feet.

"As for your friend, Yakubu," he continued, "you are welcome to him for I don't want anything more to do with him." Turning to Yakubu who was rubbing his bruised knees, he said scornfully, "Off you go with your new friends. Perhaps they'll even take you to church again!"

Yakubu gave a hitch to his torn blue shorts as he stood up. "I hope they do. But I'll tell you one thing. Their hut of prayer isn't a place of fear and evil like the one your uncle cares for in the forest. I mean to find out which is the way of truth."

"You'll find out," Buba threatened. "And when you do, don't say I didn't warn you," he shouted over his shoulder as he picked up his tattered straw hat and strode away.

The Voice from the Forest Hut

7

YAKUBU STARED AFTER BUBA UNTIL HE was out of sight. Then he grinned uneasily at the twins. "I hope he doesn't tell his uncle what I said. His uncle has a lot of power in this village, you know."

"We know," Daniya answered. "But fear of him will not catch your heart if you trust in Jesus. Jesus has far more power than the witchdoctor."

"It's not only that . . ." Yakubu followed the twins back to where they had left their scythes. Then he continued, "Buba promised me that when his uncle began to teach him the secrets of the forest hut, he would tell me all about it. Now I suppose that's all off."

"Well you just said it was a place of fear and evil, so why . . .?" Deeja began.

"Yes," Yakubu interrupted. "But I've never been *inside* the hut so I don't really know what it's all about. Buba and I went to the forest once and he showed me the hut. It was . . ." Yakubu stopped with a shudder.

"Were you afraid?" Deeja's eyes were wide.

"Truly, my heart fell down in fear," Yakubu answered. "It was because of the queer sounds coming from the hut. We turned and ran with much swiftness back to our homes. Yes, I would like to know for sure which is the true way!"

Daniya took up his scythe and began to cut the grass.

He sang quietly,

"Jesus said, 1 am the way,
I am the way, the truth and the life.
No man cometh unto the Father,
But by Me."

Deeja joined in and when they had repeated the song twice
she said, "It's all true you know, Yakubu. Jesus is the
only way to Heaven."

Yakubu nodded. "Sounds good," was all he said.

Daniya gathered the grass into a bundle and they
started for home. "Yakubu," he asked, "why is Buba
afraid of the chief?"

Yakubu shrugged. "I suppose it's because the chief is
his uncle's brother and he has already warned Buba to
stay out of mischief. It he gets into trouble too often
the chief will hinder his brother taking Buba into the
spirit worship. And Buba wants to be the next in line
for witchdoctor more than anything else."

"He really does seem terribly interested in that,"
Daniya agreed.

"Interested!" Yakubu laughed. "That's his only interest. That and Salihu."

"Salihu? Who is he?" Deeja asked.

"Salihu is Buba's four year old brother. Ever since
their mother died Buba has looked after him. Their
father has married again, but his new wife has a baby
of her own now and doesn't care much for Salihu."

"Aiya! No wonder Buba acts so unhappy." Daniya
kicked a stone out of the path and watched it land in the
grass by the roadside. "Does he live in his father's home?"

"No, he and Salihu live with his old granny in that
compound behind the village well," Yakubu answered.

They walked in silence for a while. When they reached their home Daniya said, "Will you come to Sunday School with us on Sunday, Yakubu?"

Yakubu frowned thoughtfully. "Yes, I think I will," he said at last. "That is, if my brother will let me. I live with him, you know, and help him on his farm."

"Do you have to work on Sundays too?" Deeja asked.

Yakubu nodded. "Of course! What's Sunday to us? And besides I have a peanut patch of my own which needs a lot of hoeing. I want to work hard at my farm because some day I intend to have a plough and oxen of my very own," he finished proudly.

"Good." Daniya smiled. "I know you will like my father's words on Sunday. He is going to tell a story from God's Book about a farmer who planted many seeds. And then he will tell us about the most important Seed of all which is God's Word that He plants in our hearts."

Yakubu looked interested. "I'll be sure to come," he said. "Thanks again for bringing my pig back and for helping me just now."

The next day Pastor Bako said, "Daniya, I want you and Deeja to dig some of the peanuts that are ready. You can fill two calabashes and sell them in the market."

Daniya grinned at Deeja. "Race you to the farm, Slow-One."

Deeja grabbed up her hoe and calabash and they were off. Daniya reached the farm first but in spite of that Deeja had her calabash filled before her brother.

"Now who's the slow-one?" she challenged as she watched Daniya pile the last of his peanuts into his calabash.

By the time they reached the market it was already

crowded. Tall Hausa traders had their rolls of beautiful cloth spread out on the ground. Graceful Fulani women, ornaments tinkling on their braided hair, laughed and shouted as they ladled out buttermilk to their customers. Children of all sizes ran back and forth through the crowds. Some were bartering their wares which they carried on large coloured trays on their heads. Others darted about with sharp, inquisitive eyes watching for an opportunity to snatch an unguarded penny or a bean-cake.

"People everywhere — and everywhere people," Daniya muttered good-naturedly as they pressed through the crooked alleyways between the busy stalls. Finally they found an empty spot in the vegetable section and soon were doing a brisk business.

The sun burned fiercely hour after hour. Flies swarmed and buzzed over the uncovered food. High overhead the vultures soared and waited hungrily for the time to begin their job of cleaning up the market.

At last the peanuts were all sold and Daniya said, "Let's get a drink at the well before we go home."

Deeja agreed and followed her twin out behind the market stalls towards the well. There were some children playing near the well and just then one small boy ran out of the group and climbed quickly up on the wide cement curbing of the open well. He stood up and laughed daringly down at the suddenly quiet children.

"Oh!" Deeja gasped. "He'll fall in."

Without a word Daniya dropped his empty calabash and raced toward the child who was turned slightly away from him.

"Dear Jesus, help me to reach him before he sees me," Daniya prayed. But just as he reached the well the other children saw him and began to scream in excitement. The little boy tried to turn and tottered alarmingly. Daniya gave a final leap and caught the child just as he fell backwards. Daniya held on grimly. "Deeja!" he called.

"I'm here," Deeja panted as she reached his side and helped pull the now screaming child to safety.

"Hush, hush," Deeja comforted him as she held him close. "You are all right now. I'll take you to your mother."

Daniya wiped the perspiration from his face with a trembling hand. "Kai! That was close. A small moment more and . . ."

Deeja smiled at him over the child's head. "I was praying hard."

"So was I," Daniya said. "God certainly answered us too." Turning to the staring children he said, "You are all too small to climb up on the well. Don't you know that?"

"*We* know it," piped up one sturdy little fellow of about five. "But Salihu says he can do it because he's different."

"Salihu?" Deeja tried to look at the child's face but he only pressed his tangled curls more tightly against her and continued to sob.

"Why does he think he is different?" asked Daniya.

"He says since his uncle is the witchdoctor, nothing can harm him," two or three children answered at once.

Daniya shook his head. "Salihu is mistaken. He could have fallen into that well and drowned just like any of the rest of you could. You must watch him from now on and never play near here again. Now take us to his home."

With the excited children running and shouting ahead of them, the twins made their way towards a nearby compound. Buba was standing inside the entrance hut. He was just handing some money to an old man dressed in a homespun gown that clung in tatters to his wizened body. The man clutched greedily at the money with a hand that lacked two fingers. His shifty eyes slid away from Daniya's hurriedly as he shuffled past him.

Buba turned on the noisy crowd impatiently. "Be quiet," he shouted. "What——" he stopped suddenly as he saw Deeja making her way towards him with Salihu in her arms. "What's happened to Salihu?" he asked roughly. "Is he hurt?"

"No, he's all right now." Deeja put Salihu down in front of Buba. Salihu clung to his brother's legs and began to scream again.

"He stood up on the edge of the well and nearly fell in," Deeja explained.

"The well!" Buba sat down limply. He fished around in his pocket and found a sugar lump which he gave to Salihu. Salihu stopped screaming at once and grinned triumphantly through his tears at the other children.

"He caught him. He caught him," chanted the children, pointing to Daniya. "He caught him or Salihu would have fallen into the well."

"Yes, Buba," Daniya said. "As we were going to the well we saw Salihu climb up on the edge and stand there. I ran and caught him just as he fell. Deeja helped me pull him back up."

"We prayed and Jesus helped us reach him in time," Deeja added. "We were nearly too late."

Buba glanced from one to the other. Then he looked down at his little brother. His voice was hoarse as he said, "Why did you do it, Salihu? You know I've told you never to climb on the well."

Salihu hung his head. "Our uncle is the witchdoctor, he wouldn't let me fall in the well," he said stubbornly.

Buba frowned. "You small bit of silliness," he said, crossly. "Our uncle certainly couldn't help you when he wasn't even at home. If I ever catch you playing near the well again I will whip you and lock you in with the chickens for the whole day."

Salihu's lower lip began to quiver again and Daniya said hastily, "Come on, Deeja. We must go home."

Buba stood up. "Thanks," he began uncertainly. "I . . ."

"It's all right." Daniya smiled. "We are very glad we were in time. Goodbye."

A few yards from the compound the twins looked back. Buba was kneeling beside his little brother. Salihu's arms were around his neck and their heads were close together. Neither of the twins spoke until they had each taken a long drink from the dripping bucket at the well. Then Daniya said, "Buba is a bully and he is full of meanness at times, but . . ."

"He loves his small brother," Deeja finished softly.

Daniya nodded. "Yes, and that's something. Without doubt that's a very *big* something!"

Early the next morning Daniya got ready for Sunday School. Then he and Toma started out for Yakubu's home. Along the way Daniya told Toma all about the fight between Buba and Yakubu and about little Salihu.

When they reached Yakubu's home they found a crowd of men sitting in the entrance hut. The angry discussion they were having stopped abruptly as the boys entered the hut and greeted them. When Daniya asked for Yakubu the men looked at them suspiciously, but an older man, who looked a bit like Yakubu, motioned impatiently towards the inside door and told them to go on in.

Inside the compound they again asked for Yakubu. Three women who were grinding corn stopped their work and looked at the boys fearfully. Then they pointed to a small hut that was behind the main circle of huts.

"Something has happened," Toma said in a low voice. "There is some big trouble here."

"Yes," Daniya whispered, following on Toma's heels towards the small hut. "Trouble and fear are both sitting in this home. I wonder what has caused it."

Just then they saw Yakubu. He was hunched on a low tree stump with his head in his hands. He was staring blindly at his pig stretched out on the ground.

The boys gazed in horror at the pig. The pig that only two days ago had won the prize for health and fitness was now lying at Yakubu's feet —— dead!

"What happened?" gasped Daniya.

Stark fear shone in Yakubu's eyes as he looked at them. "I should never have promised to go to church with you," he said. "It has made the spirits angry. And this," he pointed to the pig, "is their answer. Truly, the voice from the forest hut has spoken."

Buba's Triumph

8   IN SILENT SYMPATHY THE TWO BOYS squatted on the ground near Yakubu. 'If this had happened to Golden Garba my heart would be spoiled just like Yakubu's,' Daniya thought, 'But I wouldn't be full of fear like he is. How dreadful to have both misery and terror join together in your heart!'

"When did your pig get sick?" Toma asked presently.

"Sick!" Yakubu exclaimed. "He wasn't sick at all. Last night when I locked him in he was full of health. And when I opened his hut this morning he was dead."

"But what makes you think the forest hut had anything to do with it?" Daniya asked. "Just because you said you would come to church that . . ."

"Didn't my brother send word to the witch doctor this morning," Yakubu interrupted unhappily. "And didn't he send back saying the spirits of the forest hut were angry because I had gone to hear the 'Jesus Words' and was planning on going again!"

"Then Buba must have told his uncle what you said on Friday." Daniya frowned thoughtfully, then he continued, "Yakubu, I'm sure a human being has had his hand in this. Won't you come and talk it over with my father?"

"No," Yakubu said, shaking his head slowly. "I have promised not to have anything more to do with you. I am surprised that my brother allowed you to come in. See, he is coming now to send you away."

The boys looked up, and saw the man who had motioned them into the compound coming towards them. His face looked stern and unfriendly as he said, "I think you boys had better leave now if Yakubu has finished telling you that he will have nothing more to do with you 'Jesus' followers'. You have brought enough trouble on us as it is."

"We're very sorry about Yakubu's pig," Daniya said, standing up and looking frankly at the man. "We will pray and ask Jesus to help us clear up this mystery. Then perhaps Yakubu will really believe that the 'Jesus Way' is the only way to Heaven."

When the boys were out on the road leading to the church Daniya said, "What do you think happened to the pig, Toma?"

"I think it was given some poison," Toma answered. "The people in our village have many kinds of poison, you know. And there is one sly old man who is an expert at mixing and making poisons from plants and trees. His name is Gyambo and they say he works with the witch doctor too, although no one seems to know for sure."

"Gyambo" (ulcer) Daniya mused aloud. "It mustn't be very pleasant to have such a name. I wonder why he was called that?"

"My father says the people began to call him that when he was a young boy. It was because he had a bad ulcer on his hand. The ulcer lasted a long long time and he lost two fingers before his hand finally healed."

"Lost two fingers!" Daniya stopped suddenly and stared at Toma. "Say, is he a wizened up little man with eyes that jump away from you?"

"Yes," Toma laughed as they started on again. "Have you seen him?"

"I saw Buba giving him some money just yesterday," Daniya whispered hurriedly, for they had reached the church. "Perhaps Buba was paying Gyambo for the poison that killed Yakubu's pig. We must tell father about this as soon as we can after church."

But later when the boys had told Pastor Bako the story and urged him to tell the chief he only shook his head sadly. "No, boys, we haven't any proof yet. Buba would probably say he was paying Gyambo for some rope, since everyone knows Gyambo makes his living by selling rope. And of course that *may* be the truth of the matter although I am inclined to believe, like you do, that it was a far more shady transaction."

"But can't we do something, Father?" protested Deeja, who had been listening closely to the boys' story.

"Yes," answered her father, smiling. "We can and must pray very earnestly that God will bring all these 'hidden things of darkness' out into the light."

The next day the twins and their mother began preparing for another Bible club meeting.

"Where shall we have it this time, Mother?" Deeja asked. "Only Toma and Binta and Dauda and Hassen will come to our house. The other children are still afraid of Buba's threats."

"I think we should go ahead and prepare the lessons. Without doubt God will show us where to have it by Friday," their mother encouraged them.

On Wednesday evening Binta came over to learn a new chorus which she was to teach the children at the Bible club. "I do hope the boys and girls from our class will come," Deeja said with a sigh.

Binta finished copying the chorus and put it carefully in her new Bible. Then she said, "Fear will catch the children if you ask them to come to your home, just like it caught me before Jesus came to live in my heart. I think we should have it in the school yard or some place in the open. Oh! I know," she jumped up excitedly. "Mother wants Toma and me to gather shea-butter nuts on Saturday. Why don't we ask all the boys and girls to come to the forest and gather nuts on Friday afternoon and then have the Bible club there."

Deeja's face brightened. "Would there be time for both?" she asked.

"Well, even if we didn't gather many nuts, Toma and I could always finish them on Saturday."

"Let's go and tell mother and the boys," Deeja said, jumping to her feet. "I think it is a perfect plan."

When the others heard the plan they agreed that it was worth trying.

"Will you be able to come too, Mother?" Daniya asked.

Mrs. Bako smiled at the eager faces. "I could go. But I think perhaps I won't be needed this time. Binta will teach the new chorus and Deeja can give her little object lesson on the peanut. Toma has the memory verse and you could give the lesson this time, Daniya, couldn't you?" she asked, "It's the story of the prodigal son."

Daniya looked a bit doubtful. But his mother encouraged him by saying he had two nights left in which to study the lesson, so he agreed to try.

This time their plans ran smoothly. The children loved to pick shea-butter nuts and all agreed eagerly to help Binta and Toma. By four o'clock on Friday afternoon the forest rang with the merry shouts of the boys and girls. The boys climbed the trees and shook down the dark brown nuts while the girls dodged nimbly here and there filling their golden brown calabash bowls.

"Time's up," shouted Daniya presently.

"But there are still more nuts in this tree," called one of the boys. "Why not finish them?"

"We have something else planned," Toma answered. "Come over here and sit down under this tree."

Laughing and tumbling the boys and girls finally settled down in front of Daniya. Their dark eyes glowed expectantly as they waited for him to begin.

"You know what happened when we tried to have a Bible club at our home," Daniya began. "So today we thought we would have one here in the forest where no one can bother us."

"Yauwa! Splendid!" the children were enthusiastic.

"Can we have one here every week?" Ibrahim, a sturdy nine year old demanded.

"Would you come?" Daniya asked them.

"Yes, yes," they chorused.

"All right," Daniya said. "We'll plan on that. But now we had better begin."

Everything went along well. The children learned the chorus quickly and sang it lustily. They repeated the memory verse over and over again. When it came Deeja's turn she held up her closed hand. "I've got something in this hand that no one has ever seen. And when we've finished with it no one will ever see it again. Do you believe me?" she asked, smiling.

"I don't," declared Markus, a wiry young scamp perched unsteadily on a high tree stump. "Because *you* must have seen it when you took it in your hand."

Deeja shook her head. "No, I haven't seen it either. Doesn't anyone believe me?"

"I do." Juma, a thin little girl with weak eyes, answered timidly.

Deeja looked at her and smiled warmly. "Thank you, Juma," she said. Then she opened her hand and showed them a peanut. She explained that it was the nut inside that no one had ever seen. "Now," she said breaking open the peanut, "since Juma believed me I'm going to let her eat it for me. Then no one will ever see it again."

Juma ate the peanut amidst the shouts and delighted laughter of the children. Then Deeja explained that we must all believe in the Lord Jesus and accept Him into our hearts by faith even if we cannot see Him with our eyes.

Daniya held the interest of the group from the very beginning of his story. The late afternoon sunshine flickered through the swaying branches and danced over the intent upturned faces. Birds twittered and fluttered busily from tree to tree. The many coloured lizards slithered over and around the children's feet, quite unnoticed.

"And," Daniya concluded, "just as the father welcomed home his lost son, so God will welcome you if . . ."

"It's a lie!" The sudden angry words cut through the air like the sharp swish of a scythe.

"Buba!" someone shouted and instantly all was confusion.

Buba stepped from behind a shea-butter tree and held up his hand. "Yes, it's me. And I'm warning you right now that the owner has entered the forest hut. When I go

69

and tell him that you are listening to the lies of these Useless-Ones, he will surely work his medicine on you."

"Don't be afraid," Daniya called, as the frightened boys and girls began to run towards home. "God is more powerful than the owner of the forest hut."

But fear had caught at the hearts of the children and put wings to their feet. Soon they were all out of sight. Even Buba had disappeared. The twins looked at their four companions in despair.

"We may as well give up," Daniya flopped down on the grass.

"That Buba is the meanest boy I've ever known," declared Deeja indignantly. "He spoils things for us every time."

Binta was almost in tears. "And everything was going so well," she mourned. "I'm sure Juma was nearly ready to follow the 'Jesus Way'."

Hassen's long rather gloomy face was thoughtful. He said slowly, "I think Ibrahim wants to follow Jesus too. He told me that he wasn't going to listen to Buba any more."

Toma sat down beside Daniya. With a twig he began to gently tease an inquisitive little lizard that kept running up close to his feet. Finally he said, "It isn't only their fear of Buba, mostly it's the fear of the curse from the forest hut that snatches away their sense. We must prove to them that Jesus is more powerful than the owner of the forest hut."

"Tell you what!" Daniya sat up suddenly shedding his mood of discouragement. "Let's go to the forest hut on our way home. We'll take a peek inside it. Then we can tell the kids all about it and perhaps they won't be so afraid."

"Would you dare go *in* it?" Dauda's voice rose in a squeak of dismay as he asked the question.

"Yes," Daniya smiled. "Here is a verse to make you brave, Dauda. Father taught it to me once when I was afraid. '. . . greater is He that is in you, than he that is in the world'."

They all repeated the words solemnly. Then Deeja said, "Let's pray and ask Jesus to help us before we go."

When they rose to their feet they quickly divided out the shea-butter nuts into bags that Toma had brought. The boys lifted the bags to their heads and the girls carried the empty calabashes.

It was a quiet little procession that trudged along the homeward way. At the turn off to the forest hut Toma said, "We had better leave our loads here. If the owner of the forest hut *is* there he might chase us away and — I don't want to lose any of the nuts in our haste," he finished, grinning.

"I don't believe he is there at all," Daniya lowered his bag to the ground and wiped the perspiration from his forehead. "I am sure I saw Buba's uncle get in the lorry going to Hill Town this morning. Buba was just trying to scare the kids with his lies."

They started out once more. But as they rounded a bend in the path Toma, who was in the lead, stopped suddenly. "Sh—sh," he whispered. "There is Buba up ahead."

The others crowded close and stared in amazement. Buba was crawling along the edge of the trail on his hands and knees. His face was twisted with terror as he searched frantically in the grass. As he came nearer they heard him mutter, "Where can it be? I've *got* to find it."

The Lost Charm

9   "COME ON," DANIYA RAN FORWARD, the others following close behind. "What have you lost, Buba? Shall we help you look for it?" Daniya asked.

Buba sat back on his heels and glared at Daniya. "What business is it of yours what I've lost? No, I don't want help from any Useless-Ones."

Daniya noticed that Buba's hands were trembling, as he once again began to part the grass and glance hopelessly around him.

"It will soon be dark," Daniya urged. "Tell us what it looks like and we will help you find it."

Buba looked up. All around them the evening shadows were closing in. Suddenly he shivered. "All right," he growled. "It is my uncle's leather charm. It is a very important one that he wears on his arm when he needs special protection. I just borrowed it for the afternoon while he was away and now . . ."

"I thought you said he was in the hut," Deeja accused.

"Never mind," Daniya silenced her with a look. "Everyone scatter along here and look for the charm."

The children searched the grass thoroughly on each side of the road, but they couldn't find the charm. Finally they had to give up as it was getting too dark to see.

"I'm sorry," Daniya told Buba. "Perhaps we can come back tomorrow and help you look for it."

"Don't bother," Buba answered ungraciously. "I'll think of something to tell my uncle." He turned abruptly and ran towards home. His long legs covered the ground quickly and he was soon out of sight.

The others all agreed that it was now too late to visit the forest hut and they hurried after Buba down the fast darkening trail.

"Buba could have offered to help carry our nuts," Hassen grumbled good-naturedly when they reached the turn off and picked up the sacks once more.

"I think the fear that Buba is carrying is much heavier than a bag of shea-butter nuts," Daniya said.

"Without doubt," Toma agreed, falling into line behind Daniya. "For truly, Buba's uncle is a man of small mercy."

The next afternoon the twins rushed at their chores with such haste that their mother was amazed. Deeja, her water pot on her head, trotted back and forth from a nearby well until she had filled the huge clay water pot that stood in one corner of the kitchen. Then she began to grind the guinea corn into flour in preparation for their Sunday dinner.

A little later, Daniya peered into the grinding hut. "I've finished my work, Deeja. Aren't you ready yet?"

Deeja gave a final heavy swish with her grinding stone. Then she sat back on her heels and wiped the perspiration from her face. "No," she answered. "Boys always have easy jobs to do so it is not a thing of wonder that you have finished so quickly."

"Easy!" Daniya scoffed. "I've already fixed the grass fence at that broken spot, cleaned out the corn bin and cut all the grass out there behind the goat hut." He thrust his hands in front of her eyes. "Look at that for a blister. Easy huh!"

Deeja grinned, as she began her grinding again. "Well, anyway, I'll soon be finished here. Are we going to the forest hut?"

"Yes," Daniya said. "But first I thought we should get Toma and Binta and tell Buba we will help him look for his charm again."

Deeja's brows wrinkled in a troubled frown. "Do you think we should? After all we know his charm isn't any good and . . ."

"*We* know it hasn't any power, but Buba doesn't," Daniya reminded her. "And perhaps by being helpful to him we can change his ways a bit."

"All right," Deeja agreed. "Tell Binta to call for me. You boys go ahead and we'll catch up to you later on."

Daniya followed the narrow path that wound its way in and out among the crowded compounds. High in the sky the sun blazed fiercely. Its burning rays touched Daniya's tight black curls and felt like a hot blanket on his shoulders where his blue shirt was beginning to cling damply.

Toma was cleaning out his little grass-roofed pigeon hut when Daniya arrived. "Greetings on your work," Daniya said. "Are you nearly finished?"

Toma lifted a friendly pigeon from his shoulder and put it down near the grain he had scattered on the ground. Then he stood up and brushed the dust from his clothes. "I'm ready," he said. "What do you want to do?"

When Daniya told him his plan Toma agreed to go with him. Binta ran off to get Deeja and the boys headed for Buba's home.

"I hope Buba is at home and will be a little more

pleasant than he was last night," Daniya said.

Toma shook his head. "If his uncle has come back I'm afraid Buba will be in trouble. My heart always fell down in fear whenever his uncle came to visit my father. He has such a wicked wrinkled face. It is like the face of an old vulture that knows many things——and all of them evil."

"Aiya!" Daniya sighed. "It will truly be hard for Buba to become a follower of Jesus."

Toma stopped in his tracks and stared at Daniya. "You don't mean to say you are hoping to win *Buba* out of his darkness?"

"Of course," Daniya smiled ruefully. "I know it will not be easy. But after all we still have the 'whatsoever verses' you know."

"What are they?" Toma asked.

Daniya had just finished explaining about the verses when they reached Buba's home. An old woman, wizened and frail, sat on a low stool before an open fireplace made out of three large stones. She was stirring a huge pot of brew. From the strong smell the boys knew at once that she was cooking the weekly supply of guinea corn beer.

She stared at the boys curiously when they asked for Buba. "That one!" She spat on the ground and with one foot pushed some dirt over the spittle. "He was away early this morning even before the first sounds came from the women's grinding stones. Took the child with him, he did. May he drink trouble for his foolishness when the small one cries for his food!"

"Did he say where he was going?" Daniya asked.

"Would he raise his voice like the rooster in the early

dawn when he sneaks out without bringing me any firewood———not even one stick? I had to get it all myself," she muttered, glaring resentfully at the boys as if they were somehow to blame.

"I'm sure he's gone to the forest to hunt for the charm," Daniya said, as the boys left the compound, glad to get away from the strong smell of the beer and the old woman's complaining.

"Yes, and it doesn't look as if his uncle has returned yet," Toma sounded relieved.

"If we hurry perhaps we can take a look at the forest hut after we help find the charm," Daniya said.

Toma shook his head. "Not if Buba is with us. He would never let us enter it."

The boys hurried along the path that led to the forest. To their surprise they found Deeja and Binta already waiting for them under the big silk-cotton tree at the forest edge. The girls were munching on long pieces of sugar cane.

"Slow snails," they teased. "Two footed creatures that travel as slowly as chameleons need no food for the road."

"Hand it over," Daniya demanded, as he saw the extra pieces in Deeja's hand.

"Come and get it," Deeja called and the girls were off like a flash. The boys soon overtook them and after a merry scuffle took possession of their own pieces of sugar cane.

"Ummm," Toma bit off a large piece. "This watery sweetness is just what I need to give me strength."

"I wonder if that is why God says His Word is sweet to our taste. Not only because it is pleasant to read, but because it gives us strength to follow him," Deeja said.

"I think so," Daniya said. "And our verse for Sunday School tomorrow is one of joy too. Let's all say it together. '. . . ask and ye shall receive, that your joy may be full' John 16. 24."

The challenging words rang out cheerfully in the peaceful forest startling a little deer that was grazing in the shade of a large rock. The deer bounded away on swift feet. Two young monkeys high in a locust bean tree gazed at the children with bright inquisitive eyes and scolded them loudly as they passed.

When the children reached the spot where the charm had been lost they looked for Buba but he was nowhere in sight.

After searching again for the missing charm without success Daniya said, "Let us go to the forest hut now. Perhaps Buba found his charm and has gone home by the other trail."

Toma looked doubtful. "We can go to the hut, but if Buba is there I'm sure we won't get inside it."

"Well, at least we'll see the outside of it," Daniya said. "Come on, you lead the way, Toma. I'm anxious to see this hut for myself."

Toma led the way plunging quickly into what seemed a tangle of tall grass and vines. There were grunts and sighs of exasperation as his companions stumbled over stumps and became entangled in the vines but Toma paid no heed. At last he dropped to his knees and parted the grass in front of him. The others slipped down beside him and peered through the opening.

Before them lay a small clearing. In the very centre of it stood a small mud hut. Its grass roof was covered with old bones, pieces of broken calabashes and a few tattered rags. On the mud wall and black weather beaten door were large white splashes of dried gruel. Two tall palm trees held lonely vigil on either side of the little hut. Their jagged fronds rattled and creaked as if in grim warning to all who would intrude into their domain.

Suddenly Toma stiffened. "What's that?" he whispered. The others sat motionless staring at each other with wide eyes. Clearly and distinctly it came again. A low moan of pain——or was it fear?

Inside the Forest Hut

10 "THE FOREST HUT HAS SOMEONE IN ITS clutches!" Binta gasped. Her teeth were chattering and she pulled frantically at Deeja's restraining hand. "Come on, let's run home, Deeja, before it catches us."

"No." Daniya spoke quietly. He struggled to keep his voice steady as he continued. "I don't like it any more than you do, but let us pray first."

Crowding close to each other they all bowed their heads. Daniya prayed earnestly, "Dear God, please take away our fear. We know you are more powerful than the evil one. Help us to be brave and show us what to do, for Jesus' sake, Amen."

As they raised their heads Deeja suddenly exclaimed, "Buba!"

"What about him?" Toma asked. "We . . ." he stopped abruptly as the low moan came again.

"Perhaps it is Buba who is hurt," Deeja faltered. "Shouldn't we go and see?"

Daniya sprang to his feet. "Yes, that last groan seemed to come from behind the hut. I'm going to see who it is."

Toma got up slowly. Then with his chin set determinedly he followed Daniya.

"Let's go too," Deeja said, pulling a reluctant Binta after her.

They circled the hut cautiously. Suddenly Daniya broke

into a run towards a form lying under a shea-butter tree near the edge of the clearing. "It's Buba, "he called. "Come on."

Buba slowly opened pain-filled eyes and stared at the anxious faces bent over him. He tried to moisten his dry lips. "Salihu," he whispered. "Find Salihu."

"We'll look for him in a minute," Daniya promised. He turned to Deeja. "Where is the gourd of water you brought?"

"It's back where we were sitting, I'll get it." Deeja was off with a bound.

After Buba had taken a long drink from the water gourd Daniya asked, "What happened, Buba? Where are you hurt?"

Buba's face twisted with pain as he tried to move his position. "It's my foot," he said. "I went up this tree for some shea-butter nuts. Then I thought I heard my uncle coming. I leaned too far out on a branch and it broke. I don't think my foot is broken, but it hurts too much to walk on it. I told Salihu to stay beside me and he did for ever so long. But a little while ago I dozed off and when I woke up he was gone. Do find him quickly before the sun falls."

"There's a storm coming too," Binta said, pointing to the sky where black clouds were piling up rapidly.

Daniya gave a low whistle. "Kai! that storm is coming in a hurry. Two had better run for help as fast as possible."

"I'll go," Toma offered. "Me too," Binta said.

"Hurry then," Daniya urged. "Tell my father. He will know what to do."

With an anxious look at the angry scurrying clouds, Toma and Binta sped away. Daniya and Deeja searched the forest all around the clearing, but there wasn't any sign of little Salihu.

A sudden blinding flash of lightning, followed instantly by a rumbling roaring crash of thunder, made the twins rush back to Buba. "Come on, Buba," Daniya panted. "Deeja and I will help you into the hut, then I'll look for Salihu again."

Buba drew back, his eyes dark with fear. "No, no, I won't go in there. My uncle told me that no one but the owner of the hut can go in there and live."

"Jesus will protect us," Daniya assured him. "He has more power than the owner of the forest hut."

Buba shook his head unconvinced.

Suddenly Deeja had an idea. "Did you find your charm, Buba?" she asked.

"Yes, here it is," he pushed up his torn shirt sleeve as he spoke and showed them the band around his arm.

"Does it have power to keep you from harm?" Deeja continued.

"Of course it does," Buba answered, "but . . ."

"Well, why didn't it then?" Deeja demanded. "If we hadn't come along you might have been here for days before you were found."

"I suppose your God keeps you from all trouble?" Buba growled.

"He never promised that He would," Daniya spoke up. "But He has promised to be with us in trouble and never leave us or forsake us."

"And, Buba," Deeja had to raise her voice above the scream of the wind that whipped and tore furiously at the tall palm trees, "just as your charm didn't have any power to keep you from harm, neither has that hut over there any power to hurt you. So come *on*!"

Buba still hesitated, but at that moment a mighty gust of wind shook loose a shower of shea-butter nuts upon their heads and the rain poured down upon them. The twins half carrying and half pulling got the reluctant Buba over to the hut. Daniya kicked wide the half open door and the three tumbled inside.

The slashing rain was coming down in torrents now. Fortunately it was not coming toward the door so they were able to leave it open a bit for light in the windowless hut. The twins glanced curiously around the room. In one corner was a fireplace upon which sat a small black cooking pot. A pile of dry wood lay nearby.

"What's that?" Deeja pointed to what looked like a heap of rags and feathers lying near the far wall.

"We'll see," Daniya stood up.

Buba's face turned a greyish hue, as he said fiercely, "Don't you dare touch anything. It's bad enough being in here without us meddling with things."

"It won't hurt to look at it," Daniya said, stepping nearer and peering into the dimness. The next instant he gave a startled exclamation and began tossing the rags aside.

"It's Salihu," he cried.

"Salihu!" Buba's voice cracked on a rising note of fear and dread. "Is he dead?"

"Dead?" Of course not," Daniya answered. "He is sleeping the sleep of a small boy full of tiredness." Very gently, so as not to awaken him, Daniya lifted the child and put him down beside Buba.

Buba looked at Salihu in a daze of relief, mingled with amazement. "I don't understand it," he muttered.

"What don't you understand?" Deeja asked.

"Why did my uncle tell me that only the owner of the forest hut could enter it and live? Salihu has been here quite safely all this time and we are all still alive, too."

"The witchdoctor always tells the people things like that to keep them in fear so they will obey his orders," Daniya explained. "Look at this!" He went over and from the bundle of rags he picked up what appeared to be a skirt made of rags, feathers and broken pieces of calabashes.

"When the witchdoctor puts this on and dances around, the bits of calabashes clash together and make a great noise," Daniya continued. "And this is the mask he wears." Daniya took up a small cow skull complete with long curled horns. Queer dabbings of black clay gave the whole thing a weird sinister appearance.

"Ugh," Deeja shivered. "It looks horrible, Daniya, put it down."

"Gruesome, isn't it," Daniya agreed. But instead of putting it down he suddenly slipped it over his head.

"Look, Buba," he said, "this thing has no power at all in itself. The spirit men just wear things like this to scare our people."

Buba rubbed his sore foot and stared anxiously at Daniya. "How can you be sure?"

Daniya took off the mask and placed it on the pile of rags. Then he came over and sat down beside Buba. The rain was still coming down in a heavy stream, but the sound was muted by the grass roof.

Deeja's head was resting on her hand. Her eyes were closed and Daniya knew she was praying. He turned towards Buba, as he answered, "I'm sure because Jesus lives in my heart. And He has said in His Book, '. . . he that followeth me shall not walk in darkness, but shall have the light of life'. The way of the witchdoctor is the way of darkness, Buba."

"What does a Use . . ." Buba stopped and started over again. "What does a pastor's son know about the way of the witchdoctor?" Buba couldn't keep the scorn out of his voice.

"Our father was a witchdoctor before he gave his heart to Jesus Christ, and he has explained it to us," Daniya said.

"Your father was a witchdoctor!" Buba repeated in surprise. "And he left it to became a preacher?"

Deeja looked up. "Yes, he did. And now he is God's messenger which is far better than being Satan's slave."

"My uncle makes lots of money as the witchdoctor," Buba said. "And he said I could soon join him and get some money too."

"Getting money by deceiving people will never make you happy," Daniya declared. "And it certainly won't help you when it's time to die."

Buba shifted his foot uneasily. "No," he admitted grudgingly. "Money isn't much good when it comes time to die. Like old Yarima, who used to help my uncle. He died a few months ago. He had many goats and much wealth, but I saw him the day he died and his eyes were full of fear."

Daniya nodded. "The road of the forest hut will only end in fear and darkness, Buba. Your uncle has deceived you because he himself has been deceived. But now that you have discovered the truth, surely you will not agree to follow the way of lies any longer!"

Buba didn't answer. He just sat there staring at the ugly skull mask and the heap of rags. After a while he glanced down at his little brother, sleeping so peacefully beside him, and shook his head, bewildered.

The twins began to sing softly,
"I'm the resurrection and the life.
He that believeth in Me though he were dead
Yet shall he live, yet shall he live.
And whosoever liveth and believeth in Me
Shall never, never die!"

Buba stirred, impatiently. "How can you sing anything so silly like that bit about never dying. Of course we all have to die."

"Our bodies die," Daniya agreed. "But if you accept the Lord Jesus Christ into your heart as your own Saviour, Buba, when you die your spirit — that is the real you inside your body — will go straight to Jesus. And you will live with Him for ever and ever."

A sudden longing shone for an instant in Buba's eyes. Then he dropped his head and muttered, "That's all right for preacher's kids, but I don't suppose it includes people like me."

Deeja let out her breath in a long sigh as she said, "God's Book says that whosoever will may come, Buba. And that certainly *does* mean you."

"But there's something else," Buba said, squirming unhappily. "It's about — Yakubu's pig, I . . ."

"You paid to have it poisoned, didn't you?" Daniya said.

Buba gasped. "How did you know?"

"We saw you giving money to old Gyambo and we just guessed," Deeja answered.

85

"Now I suppose you'll tell the chief," Buba said, scowling darkly.

He looked so miserable that Daniya said quickly, "No, but I'll tell you what we will do, Buba. We'll help you earn money to buy another pig for Yakubu."

Buba looked at the twins in wonder. "You will?" he asked.

The twins nodded.

Very slowly Buba rolled up his sleeve. Then slipping off the leather charm he tossed it on the floor beside the mask. "Well then," he said, "I'm through with all this business. I'll tell my uncle so, too. But I'll have to wait until my foot is better."

"Why?" Deeja asked.

Buba grinned ruefully. "Because my uncle is a man of much anger and I'll need to be able to run quickly after I tell him."

"Oh," Daniya paused, then he continued, "but, Buba, you can't stand up to your uncle in your own strength. You will need Jesus to help you."

"Didn't I just tell you I was finished with the witch-doctor's road. Isn't that enough?"

"Look, Buba," Deeja explained, "if you picked up a mango and discovered it was a bad one, by throwing it away would you satisfy your hunger?"

"Of course not," Buba answered. "I'd have to hunt until I found a good mango and then eat it."

"Well, the witchdoctor's road is the bad mango and the 'Jesus Way' is the good mango. Only the 'Jesus Way' is much sweeter than any mango you have ever tasted," Deeja finished.

"How do I get into the 'Jesus Way' then?" Buba asked, still puzzled.

Daniya smiled. "Just close your eyes, Buba, and tell Jesus that you believe He died for you. Ask Him to forgive you and tell Him that you want Him to come and live in your heart, and He will do it."

"All right," Buba agreed, closing his eyes.

And as the rain poured down relentlessly upon the little hut Buba gave his heart into the keeping of the Saviour.

Just as the three raised their heads there was a shout from outside. "Here they come," Deeja exclaimed.

"Won't the school kids be surprised when we tell them we have seen all the secrets of the forest hut," Daniya said, standing up.

"And when they hear I have found the best secret of all," Buba added thankfully.